Spaced Out

by Lisa Thompson

illustrated by Bettina Guthridge

STANLEY
THORNES

The Characters

Jed

Comet

Jed's sister

The Setting

my room

CONTENTS

CHAPTER 1

Jed in Space

Jed is space mad.
His room is filled with pictures
of space and spaceships.

There are glow-in-the-dark stars
on the walls. Planets hang
from the ceiling.

When Jed turns the light off
at night, he feels like he
is floating in space.

5

Jed spends a lot of his time
looking at space
through his telescope.

When the night sky is clear,
Jed can see the surface
of the moon.
He can see different kinds
of stars.

Jed's sister, Ali,
thinks Jed is weird
for looking up at space
all the time.

"I don't know what you think
is so interesting up there,"
Ali says.

"That's because your brain
is a vacuum," says Jed.
In space talk "vacuum" means empty.

Collecting Moon Samples

In the backyard
there is a big pile of rocks
and sand. Jed thinks
it looks like the surface
of the moon.

With his dog, Comet,
Jed spends hours collecting rock
and sand samples.
Like a real astronaut.

Jed has made his skateboard
into a moon buggy. He uses it
to collect his moon samples.

When Comet or Jed find something
they return to the spaceship. Here,
they inspect what they have found.

So far they have discovered three dog bones, a piece of limestone, two marbles and one old coin.

What Jed wants is a real piece of space rock.

CHAPTER 3

A Spaceship?

One night Jed sees something
in the sky that he has never
seen before. A big ball of light
shoots across the sky.
It's bright orange with a long tail.

It lands just behind
the back fence.

As scared as he is,
Jed knows he has to go outside
and take a look.

Jed hears noises
on the other side of the fence.

"Aliens," he thinks.

Maybe it is a spaceship
from another planet.
What if the aliens have seen Jed
looking through his telescope?
They might take him away
and throw him into a black hole.

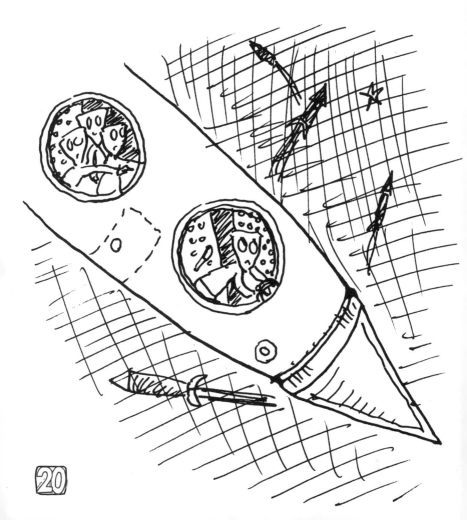

His dad has told him all about
black holes. If you fall into one,
you end up all long and thin
like a piece of spaghetti.

Maybe they are friendly aliens
and want to take him back
to their planet. He would be famous.
Then he could do whatever
he wanted to.

He would spend all his time
travelling through space
and going to new planets.

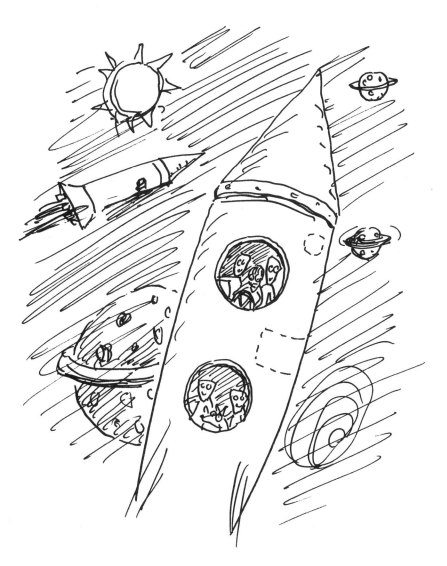

Aliens

Jed finds a hole in the fence
and bravely climbs through.

"AHHHHHHHHHHHHHHHHH!" he screams.

The alien has a moon-shaped head, long hair and two big, brown eyeballs just like his own.

Jed closes his eyes and screams again.

"Stop screaming!" the alien says.
It touches his shoulder.
Jed screams even more loudly.

"Open your eyes," it orders.

Jed peeks out of his left eye. Standing in front of him is his ... sister.

"What's wrong with you?" she asks.
"You look all spaced out,
like you've just seen an alien or
something."

Jed's Mum and Dad and sister are all staring at him. Jed's dog, Comet, is too.

"Look, Jed," says his dad,
pointing to a hole in the ground,
"a space rock has landed right here."

CHAPTER 5

Space Rock

Three scientists come to look
at the space rock.
They do all kinds of tests.

Jed and Comet sit
on the moon buggy and watch.

Finally, the scientists finish.

"Everything looks safe," they say.

One of the scientists hands
the rock to Jed. "Here Jed,
you can have it.
It's a bit of a meteorite."

Jed can't believe it.
"You mean I can keep it?" he asks.

Jed runs inside to show
the others.

"Look everyone. I get to keep
the space rock. It's a meteorite."

Be Very Careful

Later, Jed finds his sister using his telescope.

"This space stuff is so cool. There's just so much to see. Can I have a look at the meteorite?" she asks.

Jed nods.
He looks at her moon face and big,
brown eyes.

He has to be careful.
Maybe his sister
isn't a vacuum after all.

Maybe she is an alien.

GLOSSARY

alien
creature from space

astronaut
someone who
travels in space

inspect
to look at closely

meteorite
a rock from space

rock from space

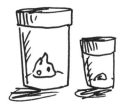

samples
small parts or pieces

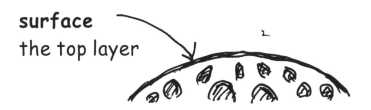

surface
the top layer

telescope
used to look at stars

vacuum
completely empty

weird
strange

Lisa Thompson

How high can you jump?

If I want, I can jump any size fence. No worries.

Why do ants have 6 legs?

Because when they got to the 'Things to Stick on Your Body' table, six ant legs were all that were left.

What is your favourite toy?

Lemon Twister — it makes you look really silly.

What is the hardest part of your day?

Looking for the keys time!

Bettina Guthridge

How high can you jump?

I don't like heights.

Why do ants have 6 legs?

So they can walk along tightropes.

What is your favourite toy?

My border collie called Tex.

What is the hardest part of your day?

When I have to be grown up.